DUDLEY SCHOOL LIBRARY
AND INFORMATION

KU-743-040

Schools Library and Information Services

S00000650378

DUDLEY PUBLIC LIBRARIES

L 46683

650378 SCH

JJ

Text copyright © Adèle Geras 2002
Illustrations copyright © Alan Marks 2002
Book copyright © Hodder Wayland 2002

Consultant: Jonathan Gorsky, The Council of Christians and Jews
Editor: Katie Orchard

Published in Great Britain in 2002
by Hodder Wayland, an imprint of
Hodder Children's Books.

The right of Adèle Geras to be identified as the
author of this Work and of Alan Marks as the
illustrator of this Work has been asserted by them in
accordance with the Copyright, Designs and Patents Act 1988.

All rights reserved. No part of this publication may
be reproduced, stored in a retrieval system, or
transmitted, in any form or by any means without
the prior permission of the publisher, nor be otherwise
circulated in any form of binding or cover other than
that in which it is published and without a similar
condition being imposed on the subsequent purchaser.

Cataloguing in Publication Data
Geras, Adèle
The Taste of Winter: A story about Hanukkah. – (Celebration stories)
1. Hanukkah – Juvenile literature 2. Children's stories
I. Title
823.9'14 [J]

ISBN: 0 7502 3657 4

Printed in Hong Kong by Wing King Tong

Hodder Children's Books
A division of Hodder Headline Limited
338 Euston Road, London NW1 3BH

CELEBRATION STORIES

The Taste of Winter

ADÈLE GERAS

Illustrated by Alan Marks

HODDER
Wayland

an imprint of Hodder Children's Books

Celebrating Hanukkah

Hanukkah is the Jewish winter festival that takes place over eight days starting in either late November or December. It is a movable feast because it is celebrated according to the dates of the Jewish calendar, which varies from year to year. Hanukkah always begins on the twenty-fifth day of a month called *Kislev*. It commemorates the victory of Judah Maccabee and his followers over the forces of the Syrian king, Antiochus, who desecrated the Temple that the Jews held sacred.

The Maccabees defeated Antiochus and took the Temple back into Jewish hands. A miracle made the very tiny amount of oil in the lamps last for eight days, and that is why Jews light one new candle for each night of the festival. They use an extra candle called a *shamash* (or servant) to light the Hanukkah ones. By the end of Hanukkah, all the candles on the Menorah (the eight-branched candelabra) are burning together.

Hanukkah is sometimes called 'The Festival of Lights'.

It is customary to eat fried foods at this time, such as potato cakes (latkes) and doughnuts. Special prayers are also said and Hanukkah songs are sung both in synagogues and in Jewish homes.

Children receive a small present on each night of the festival. A traditional gift is the little four-sided spinning-top called a dreidel, which has a letter of the Hebrew alphabet on each side: N, (*nun*) G (*gimmel*) H (*hey*) SH (*shin*). These are the initial letters for the Hebrew phrase meaning: A great miracle took place there. This refers to the Temple oil lasting for a whole week in the time of Judah Maccabee.

A Special Assembly

It was three o'clock on Friday afternoon. Miss Harris smiled at the children in her class. "Now everyone, I hope you are all ready to bring in lots of lovely things for our Winter Festivals assembly next week," she said. "Every religion has a festival at this time of year. We'll be telling the whole school about the different ways people celebrate. There's Christmas, of course, and Divali a little before that, and…"

Miss Harris turned to Naomi. "Tell everyone what the Jewish winter festival is called, Naomi."

"Hanukkah, Miss," said Naomi.

"And do you think you'll be able to bring us something for the display we're going to put up?"

"Oh, yes, Miss Harris," said Naomi. "I'll ask my mum tonight."

For the rest of the afternoon, Naomi was really excited. She couldn't stop thinking about the assembly.

At home-time, when she ran to meet her mum at the school gates, she started talking about it at once.

"Mum, *Mum!*" she said. "We're going to do a Winter Festivals assembly in front of the whole school…"

Naomi's mum smiled at her. "Hello to you, too, Naomi! Just wait five seconds before you start telling me anything. Have you had a nice day?"

Naomi said, "Sorry, Mum, but I'm *so* excited. Miss Harris has asked me to bring in something for the display. Something to do with Hanukkah."

"Start at the beginning, love. What display is this?"

Naomi told her mother all about the special assembly. "I'm the only Jewish person in the class," she explained. "So I've got to bring in something to do with Hanukkah."

"Like a Menorah, you mean?" asked Naomi's mum. "Something like that?"

The Menorah was a beautiful candelabra, big enough to hold the eight Hanukkah candles, with the extra *shamash* candle in the middle. It stood on the mantelpiece in the lounge, and it was only used to hold the Hanukkah candles.

"That would be *wonderful*," said Naomi. "Are you sure you don't mind, Mum? It's made of gold, isn't it? What if something happened to it?"

Naomi's mum laughed. "No, it's made of brass. It's because I polish it up that it gleams like that. And I'll let you have a smaller Menorah we've got put away – that one is made of real silver."

"I love Hanukkah," Naomi said. "But I don't remember the whole story. I should know what happened, shouldn't I? Miss Harris will probably ask me to tell the rest of the school."

"It just so happens," said Naomi's mum, "that the Rabbi and his wife are coming to supper tomorrow. I'm sure he'd love to tell you, so why don't you ask him then? I've got to get the Sabbath meal ready now, and you should change out of your school clothes."

"That's a good idea," said Naomi. "I like Rabbi David. He's really nice and he loves telling stories."

Rabbi David Tells a Story

On Saturday night, Rabbi David and his wife, Claire, came to Naomi's house. Naomi's Mum and Claire were in the kitchen doing last-minute things to the food, while Rabbi David and Naomi's Dad waited in the lounge. Naomi waited until Rabbi David had settled down in his chair with a glass of wine.

"May I ask you something, Rabbi David?" asked Naomi. "I need it for school."

"Certainly, Naomi," he said. "Ask me whatever you want to know."

The smells coming from the kitchen were delicious. Rabbi David added, "The food smells so wonderful… you can help me take my mind off it while we wait."

"Will you tell me the story of Hanukkah? We're having a Winter Festivals assembly at school and I might have to tell the other children about it."

"It's the story of a miracle," said Rabbi David, taking a sip of wine. "Long, long ago, a Syrian king called Antiochus ruled over the Jews in their land. The Jews had their Temple to worship in – a magnificent building in Jerusalem – but Antiochus forbade them to pray there. And then he desecrated the Temple."

"What does that mean, *desecrated*?" Naomi asked, wide-eyed.

"It means he did everything he could to make the Temple not holy. Antiochus made his people bring pigs into it, and they killed the animals in the Temple as sacrifices to their own gods. Then Antiochus had statues of those gods put up in the Jewish Temple."

"What happened then?" Naomi asked.

"A brave man called Judah Maccabee and his brothers fought Antiochus and at last were surrounded in the Temple by Antiochus' soldiers. When the fighting was over, they had only enough oil to last in the Temple lamps for one day – a very small amount of oil indeed. But God was looking down on them, and He brought about a miracle.

"That first night, when the oil should have run out, there was just enough for one more day, still at the bottom of the jar. Then on the second night, the same thing happened again: the oil had not run out. For eight days and nights the oil lasted, and by then the Jews had had time to make some more." Rabbi David paused to sip his wine again.

"But what happened?" asked Naomi. "Antiochus didn't win, did he?"

"Oh, no! Antiochus was defeated and the Temple was reconsecrated – made holy all over again. Ever since, we've celebrated Hanukkah by lighting eight candles, one for every day that the oil lasted in the days of Judah Maccabee."

Rabbi David glanced around the room. "I see your Menorah up there – and a very handsome one it is, too. Menorah means 'lamp', did you know that? Hanukkah is the Jewish Festival of Lights."

"Yes, I know that," said Naomi. "But why do we eat things like doughnuts and latkes and have presents every night?"

"The food is cooked in oil. That's good for warming you up in the winter. It also reminds us of Judah Maccabee's oil. And we give children small presents to show how happy we are to remember how our Temple was returned to us." Rabbi David sniffed the air longingly.

Naomi could smell roast chicken. She felt hungry, too. "I love latkes," she said. "Once, I grated the potatoes for Mum when she made some."

"Your mother is a wonderful cook. But you know, your neighbour, Mrs Rakovsky, makes the best latkes I've ever had. You should go and visit her."

"Come and eat," said Naomi's mum. Rabbi David stood up.

"Thanks for telling me the story," Naomi said. She wished that it wasn't Mrs Rakovsky who made the best latkes. She always seemed a little crotchety and Naomi didn't like her very much. She didn't see why they had to go and see Mrs Rakovsky, but Mum always said that she was all on her own, and that they had to visit her from time to time.

"But why do I have to come?" Naomi always asked.

"She really likes seeing someone young."

Naomi couldn't understand that. If Mrs Rakovsky liked seeing her, why did she ignore her every time they visited?

After dinner, Naomi went up to her room and thought about Rabbi David's story. She would certainly have lots to tell Miss Harris and the rest of the class.

• • • • •

When Naomi woke up on Sunday morning, she remembered that tomorrow was the day she was taking the Menorah into school for the display.

She poured milk on her cereal and said, "Please, Mum, can I really not have the brass Menorah for the display? I'm sure Miss Harris will take great care of it. It wouldn't get lost or anything, I promise. It's so big and shiny, it will really stand out and everyone will notice it first."

Mum said, "I don't want give you that one, Naomi, because it used to belong to my great-grandmother and it's very precious. But wait till you see the one I've got for you. You'll like that even better. I told you, it's real silver."

Naomi sighed and helped herself to a piece of toast and started buttering it. "OK. I'll have the silver one, then."

"I'll get it out of the cupboard after breakfast. You'll like it, I'm sure."

Mrs Rakovsky

Naomi sat in Mrs Rakovsky's lounge and bit into a chocolate biscuit. Her mum had decided that, as it was nearly Hanukkah, they should drop in to wish the old lady a happy festival. Now Mum and Mrs Rakovsky were chatting away and Naomi felt bored. Then Mum started talking about the display and the Menorah, and Mrs Rakovsky turned to Naomi and smiled.

"That reminds me, I've got something for you, my dear. A little present for Hanukkah."

"A present!" Naomi felt that maybe Mrs Rakovsky was kinder than she seemed. Whatever could it be?

"Open it now, if you like," said Mrs Rakovsky, handing Naomi a small parcel.

Naomi said, "Oh, it's a *dreidel!* A little spinning top! How lovely."

"And do you know what the Hebrew letters written on it mean?" asked Mrs Rakovsky.

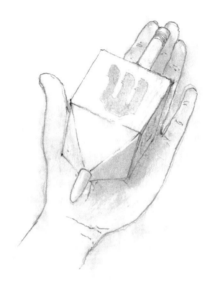

Naomi shook her head.

"The letters *nun, gimmel, hay* and *shin* stand for '*Ness gadol haya sham*', which means, 'A great miracle happened there'."

"I know about the miracle!" Naomi said. "Rabbi David told me about Judah Maccabee and the Temple and the oil. This is a lovely present. Thank you so much, Mrs Rakovsky."

"It's a pleasure," said Mrs Rakovsky. "Perhaps you could take it in for the display?"

"Oh, no, I'm taking a Menorah to school tomorrow. It's much bigger than the dreidel and it's made of silver."

"I'm sure you're right," said Mrs Rakovsky a little sadly. "A Menorah will certainly make more of an impression."

"But I do love my dreidel, really," said Naomi. She tried to think of something that would show Mrs Rakovsky how much she liked it. She added, "I wouldn't want it to get lost among all the other things in the display."

Mrs Rakovsky nodded and looked a little happier.

By the time they went home, Naomi had decided that perhaps Mrs Rakovsky was quite nice after all.

A Disappointment

On Monday morning, Naomi carried the wrapped silver Menorah carefully into her classroom. She went up to Miss Harris's desk.

"Look, Miss Harris," she said proudly. "I've brought this for the display. It's called a Menorah and I know the whole story of Hanukkah, too."

"That's excellent, Naomi. You'll be able to tell everyone on Friday, won't you? Let's see your Menorah… oh, it's beautiful! Why don't you put it on the table, and write a clear label for it…"

Naomi looked at the display table, which already had lots of things on it: fir cones and holly and crackers, and a sort of wooden triangle with candles stuck along two sides of it. The candles weren't lit, but Naomi could see how pretty it would look when there were little flames shining out…

Naomi bit her lip. It looked a bit like her Menorah and she felt suddenly disappointed. What she'd brought wasn't special any more. It seemed that other places and other religions also had candles as part of their winter celebrations.

Miss Harris said, "Is anything the matter, Naomi? You look sad."

"No, Miss," said Naomi. "It's just that I thought my Menorah would be the only thing with candles in it, that's all."

"Many religions use candles in their ceremonies, for all sorts of different reasons," Miss Harris explained. "Some of the children will be able to explain why candles are important to their own celebrations at the assembly. Often special foods are eaten at such times as well."

Naomi nodded. "Yes, we have doughnuts and special potato pancakes called latkes…" she stopped suddenly as an idea came to her. She couldn't wait till home-time to tell her mum about it.

When the bell went at quarter past three, Naomi rushed out of class and straight to where her mum was waiting.

"Mum, *Mum!*" she said. "Can we go and visit Mrs Rakovsky? I really need to speak to her. Do you think if I asked her nicely, she would…" Naomi whispered into her mum's ear, so that no one around could hear.

"Yes," said Mum. "I think she'd be thrilled to bits to be asked. Let's go and see her now."

A Hanukkah Surprise

On Friday morning, Naomi woke up very early. She was dressed in her best clothes for the special assembly long before it was time for breakfast.

When she went downstairs, Mum said, "Everything's ready, darling. Don't look so worried."

"Did you check?" Naomi wanted to know.

"Yes, I saw with my own eyes. Everything will be perfect."

The special assembly was at half past two. No one in the class had done any proper work the whole day. They'd had a rehearsal and decorated the hall and put the final touches to the display table, which had been moved from the classroom to the stage so that everyone could see it.

Naomi's whole class and Miss Harris were on stage as well. Everyone was looking at the doors, and watching the mothers and fathers, grandparents and little brothers and sisters coming in.

"Is that your granny?" whispered Inderjeet.

"No," said Naomi. "That's Mrs Rakovsky. She's our neighbour."

The piano music started playing and someone closed the doors to the hall. Naomi felt a little nervous. She hoped that she'd remember all the words she'd been learning for the last two days. She wished the butterflies in her stomach would settle down.

The special assembly was over. Everyone had spoken their piece without any mistakes at all, and the singing was loud and cheerful.

Miss Harris came to the front of the stage. "I'd like to thank you for coming to our assembly," she said. "The children have all worked very hard, and they deserve a treat. You must share it with us, too. You heard Naomi talking earlier about Hanukkah, the Jewish Festival of Lights. Mrs Rakovsky, Naomi's neighbour, has been cooking all morning, and we have some Jewish potato pancakes, called latkes, to share with you."

41

Naomi watched as her mother and Mrs Rakovsky left the room. They soon came back with two large trays, on which golden latkes were piled high. They walked about among the parents and everyone took a latke. You could see that they loved the taste. People couldn't help smiling.

"You'll have to write down the recipe for us, Mrs Rakovsky," said Miss Harris. "I'm sure everyone will want to make these at home."

"It's been a pleasure for me," said Mrs Rakovsky. "I'm so glad my friend Naomi thought of asking me to cook them. And it was good of you to let me reheat them in the canteen oven. They do have to be eaten hot."

Mrs Rakovsky smiled at Naomi and Naomi smiled back. She took a latke from the tray and closed her eyes as she bit into it. It tasted of Hanukkah.

A Recipe for Latkes

Why not try making latkes yourself? This recipe serves six people:

Grate 2 kg of potatoes. Wrap the grated potatoes in a clean tea towel and squeeze as dry as possible. Then mix potatoes and two finely-chopped onions with three eggs and enough flour or matzo meal (or a combination of both) to make a paste that looks like a thick pancake batter. Ask an adult to help you fry spoonfuls of this mixture in hot oil, and when one side is nicely golden, turn each latke over to cook the other side. Serve them hot.

Glossary

Candelabra A holder for more than one candle, often made of some precious metal.

Desecrate To do something in a place of worship which insults those people who think it is a holy place. To make something less holy.

Menorah A special Jewish candelabra. During Hanukkah, an extra candle in the Hanukkah Menorah is lit each night.

Rabbi A Jewish religious leader. He is in charge of the Synagogue and looks after his congregation.

Reconsecrate To make a place holy again. There is usually a special service that the Rabbi has to conduct.

Sabbath The Jewish Day of Rest. The Sabbath is every Saturday, which is a holy day on which work is forbidden.

Shamash The Hebrew word for 'servant'. A *shamash* candle is used to light each Hanukkah candle.

CELEBRATION STORIES

Look out for these other titles in the **Celebration Stories** series:

Coming Home by Jamila Gavin
It's almost Divali, and there's lots to do. But then Preeta goes missing – and in the world of the gods, a battle rages between good and evil. When the night grows dark, will the Divali candles light everyone safely home?

The Best Prize of All by Saviour Pirotta
Linda has spent months growing a giant pumpkin for the Harvest Festival. She knows she's going to win the prize for the biggest vegetable. But she's not the only one who wants first prize. So when Linda's pumpkin is stolen the night before the competition, she's convinced she knows who's responsible…

The Guru's Family by Pratima Mitchell
When Baljit visits the Panjab, he realizes that his family is scattered around the world – just like the stars in the night sky. So, when Guru Nanak's Birthday comes, Baljit and his cousin, Priti, use the Internet to bring everyone together.

You can buy all these books from your local bookseller, or order them direct from the publisher. For more information about Celebration Stories, write to: *The Sales Department, Hodder Children's Books, a division of Hodder Headline Limited, 338 Euston Road, London NW1 3BH.*